ZIONSVILLE PUBLIC LIBRARY

3 3946 00315 5913

P9-BYC-153

Acknowledgements

All praise belongs to Allah alone, and may Allah's blessings and peace be upon Muhammed, his family, companions and descendants. I wrote this book for my children to help them learn to love nature and to begin to contemplate Allah's signs in the world. I am especially grateful to my husband who cooks and helps with our children after a very long day of work so that I can write. *Al-Hamdulillah*.

PRESENTED BY

NURA, DENA AND HANA

PAARLBERG

2016

© DEMCO, INC.— Archive Safe

© J. Samia Mair 2010/1430 A.H. Hardback   Reprint 2012

ISBN 978-0-86037-438-1

All rights reserved. No part of this publication may be reproduced, stored in a retrieval system or transmitted by any means whatsoever, without the prior permission of the copyright owner.

MUSLIM CHILDREN'S LIBRARY

The Perfect Gift
Author: J. Samia Mair
Editor: Farah Alvi
Illustrations: Craigh Howarth
Cover/Book Design: Nasir Cadir
Coordinator: Anwar Cara

Published by
THE ISLAMIC FOUNDATION,
Markfield Conference Centre, Ratby Lane, Markfield,
Leicestershire, LE67 9SY, United Kingdom
Website: www.islamic-foundation.org.uk

QURAN HOUSE, P.O. Box 30611, Nairobi, Kenya

P.M.B. 3193, Kano, Nigeria

All enquiries to
Kube Publishing
Tel: +44(0)1530 249230, Fax +44(0)1530 249656
Email: info@kubepublishing.com
www.kubepublishing.com

A catalogue record of this book is available from British Library

Printed by Imak Ofset   Istanbul - TURKEY

The Perfect Gift

J. Samia Mair

Illustrated by Craigh Howarth

Hussey-Mayfield Memorial
Public Library
Zionsville, IN 46077

SARAH looked out of the window. She was very sad. It would soon be Eid, and she still did not have a gift for her mother.

Sarah's older brother had a gift. He bought their mother a light green scarf from her favourite store. Her older sister found a gift as well. She wrote one of their mother's favourite ayahs in calligraphy and framed it.

Sarah did not have money to buy a gift, nor did she write calligraphy. She felt that she would never find the perfect gift for her mother.

Sarah decided to take a walk in the woods behind her house. Walking among the tall trees made her forget about whatever was bothering her. She always returned home in a better mood.

6

Sarah put on her boots, coat, hat, and mittens. It had snowed during the night and a thin blanket of white covered everything for as far as she could see.

It was now late morning. The sky was brilliant blue and the sun was big and yellow. Sunlight bounced off the melting snow, making the whole world sparkle. Sarah thought that the woods had never looked more beautiful.

Sarah took her special path to the right that only she knew about.
The path led to a stream that meandered silently through the woods.

She climbed over a large tree trunk that had fallen in a thunderstorm the previous summer and headed toward a small hill in the distance. On the other side of the hill was the stream.

Suddenly, something unusual caught her attention in a small clearing off the path. Rays of sunshine pierced through the trees, shining directly on the spot. As she walked closer, she realized it was a flower — the first flower of spring.

The flower had bright orange petals, each one as large as the palm of her hand. They were smooth and shiny, and sunlight bounced off them like it bounced off snow.

The flower's two oval leaves were a tender shade of green, and the flower itself stood on a sturdy green stem. It was the most magnificent flower Sarah had ever seen. Sarah smiled and whispered to herself, "The perfect gift."

Sarah walked over to the clearing where the flower grew and bent down to pick it. Just as she was about to snap the stem, something stopped her.

She stood up and gazed at the flower. She then remembered a saying of the Prophet Muhammad, "Allah is beautiful and loves beauty."

Sarah turned around and started to run back home, leaping over the fallen log in her path. She ran past the front door of her house and headed straight for the garage.

She knew exactly what she needed but was unsure where to find everything. She quickly searched through all the boxes in the garage and looked on all the shelves.

A few minutes later, Sarah appeared from the garage with a box full of materials. She carried the box as fast as she could back to the spot where the flower grew.

Sarah immediately started her work. After what seemed like a very long time, she stood up and once again gazed at the flower. "Perfect," Sarah whispered to herself.

Sarah ran all the way home for a second time that morning. As she approached the front steps of her house, she called for her mother, baba, brother, and sister. They met her at the door.

"Follow me! Follow me!" Sarah said excitedly. Sarah's mother, baba, brother, and sister quickly put on their boots, coats, hats, and gloves and followed Sarah into the woods. They could barely keep up with her as she ran ahead of them.

"*Subhanallah!*" Sarah's mother exclaimed when she saw the flower and what Sarah had built to protect it. A little picket fence surrounded the flower. The fence was made of Popsicle sticks that she had painted and joined together with glue.

A small sign written in different coloured crayons hung on the fence from a piece of purple yarn. It read, 'Eid Mubarak. Allah's Perfect Gift to the world.'

Sarah and her family spent the rest of the morning admiring the flower and enjoying the sparkling woods. Every day, they returned to the small clearing to see the 'Perfect Gift.'

After a while, the flower's petals began to wilt and fall off. Tiny seed pods grew. At first Sarah was sad, but her mother told her not to be. The flower had lived the life that Allah had created it to live and nothing could be better than that.

The next year, on Eid ul-Adha, Sarah and her family returned to the same spot where the magnificent flower grew the year before, but it was not there.

It was too early for any flowers to grow as buds were just beginning to appear on the trees. But on one of the branches of a tall tree, they saw the most beautiful thing. A long slender icicle hung from the branch. Sunlight shone through it revealing a beautiful rainbow of colours. Sarah smiled. "Another perfect gift".

To this day, every Eid ul-Adha, Sarah and her family walk together on Sarah's special path through the woods. And every year, no matter what season it is, they find the 'Perfect Gift.'
Al-Hamdulillah.